Ms. LaGrange Is Strange!

Ms. LaGrange Is Strange!

Dan Gutman

Pictures by
Jim Paillot

HarperTrophy®
An Imprint of HarperCollinsPublishers

Ms. LaGrange Is Strange!
Text copyright © 2005 by Dan Gutman
Illustrations copyright © by Jim Paillot

Library of Congress Cataloging-in-Publication Data
Gutman, Dan
    Ms. LaGrange is strange! / Dan Gutman ; pictures by Jim Paillot – 1st Harper Tropfiy ed.
        p.   cm. – (My weird school ; #8)
    Summary: The new lunch lady at Ella Mentry school, Ms. La Grange, writes secret
messages in the mashed potatoes and tries her best to get A.J. and the other students to
eat healthy foods.
    ISBN-10: 0-06-082223-6 (pbk.) – ISBN-10: 0-06-082224-4 (lib. bdg.)
    ISBN-13: 978-0-06-082223-1 (pbk.) – ISBN-13: 978-0-06-082224-8 (lib. bdg.)
    [1. Schools–Fiction.   2. School lunchrooms, cafeterias, etc–Fiction.   3. Food–Fiction.
4. Humorous stories.]   1. Paillot, Jim, ill.   II. Title   III. Series
PZ7.G9846Mw 2005   2005005731
[Fic]–dc22   CIP
                                                                                     AC

❖
First Harper Trophy edition, 2005

Visit us on the World Wide Web!
www.harperchildrens.com

09 10 11 12 13 LP/CW 20 19 18 17 16 15 14 13 12

To Emma

Contents

A Pretty Normal Lunch

My name is A.J. and I hate school.

"Which do you hate more," my friend Ryan asked me, "school or vegetables?"

"Hmmm, that's a hard one," I said. "I really hate them both."

"I hate school more than vegetables," said our friend Michael, who never ties his shoes, "because we don't have to sit inside a vegetable all day and learn stuff."

"Good point," I agreed.

"I hate vegetables more than school," Ryan said, "because we don't have to *eat* the school."

That made perfect sense too. I couldn't make up my mind.

We were in the vomitorium. It was a pretty normal lunch at Ella Mentry School. Ryan stuck carrot sticks in his mouth and said, "Look, I'm a walrus!" Michael put a spoon on his nose, and it hung there. I dared Ryan to put pickle chips on his Tater Tots and eat them. Ryan will eat anything.

Michael dared me to shoot a straw wrapper at Andrea Young, this girl at the next table who is really annoying. The wrapper hit Andrea in the head. She screamed and knocked her apple juice on the floor.

Just at that moment, Andrea's annoying friend Emily was walking by with her tray. Emily slipped on the juice and fell on her butt. As she was falling, she knocked over a whole rack of lunch trays. *Crash!*

"Ouch!" Emily shouted. "I bumped my mouth. My tooth is loose!"

I don't know why, but when people fall on their butt, it's hilarious. Me and Ryan and Michael just about exploded trying not to laugh. Emily started crying. That big crybaby. She wasn't even hurt, and her tooth was probably loose before she fell.

Mrs. McGillicuddy, the lunch lady, came running out.

"What's going on?" she screamed. "Can't you kids behave?"

Mrs. McGillicuddy is the meanest lunch lady in the history of the world. She's always yelling at us to clean off our table, be quiet, and stop throwing food. She's no fun at all.

Mrs. McGillicuddy must not have seen the apple juice on the floor when she came running out. She slipped on it and fell on her butt too.

It's even funnier when grown-ups fall on their butts, especially mean grown-ups like Mrs. McGillicuddy. Everybody was cracking up.

"You kids are driving me crazy!" Mrs.

McGillicuddy shouted. "That's the last straw! I quit!"

She was totally wrong. There were plenty of straws right there on the lunch counter. But Mrs. McGillicuddy must not have noticed. She yanked off her plastic apron, ripped off her plastic gloves, and pulled off her lunch lady hairnet. She threw all that stuff on the floor and stomped out of the vomitorium.

I'll tell you, there are a lot of crazy grown-ups at Ella Mentry School. But this was the first time I ever saw one of them actually *go* crazy, live and in person. It was cool.

Miss Lazar, our custodian, came over

with a mop. I feel sorry for her. Every time some kid spills something, she has to clean it up.

"I love cleaning up messes!" Miss Lazar said, mopping the apple juice off the floor. Miss Lazar is bizarre!

When all the excitement was over, Ryan put a carrot stick in his nose and ate it (the carrot stick, not his nose). Michael made a sculpture out of tuna salad. I threw a cookie to Ryan, and he caught it in his mouth.

Like I said, it was a pretty normal lunch.

A Special Guest

Finally it was time for recess. Mr. Klutz, our principal, says kids today don't get enough exercise. There should be recess all day long, if you ask me. We should have school for half an hour, instead of the other way around. Then we'd get lots of exercise.

"That was cool when Mrs. McGilli-cuddy quit," Ryan said as we climbed the monkey bars.

"Yeah," I said. "I guess they'll have to find a new lunch lady."

"Where are they gonna find a new lunch lady?" asked Michael.

"Mr. Klutz will put an ad in the paper," Ryan said.

"That takes too long," Michael said. "We need a lunch lady *tomorrow*."

NEEDED!
LUNCH LADY
WHERE:
ELLA MENTRY SCHOOL
WHEN:
NOW!
CALL MR. KLUTZ

Michael was right. If Mr. Klutz didn't get a new lunch lady tomorrow, there would be no lunch tomorrow. And if there was no lunch tomorrow, we would starve and die. My friend Billy who lives around the corner told me that if people have no food, they get so hungry they'll even eat dirt.

"Maybe our moms can be lunch ladies," Michael said.

I don't think that's gonna happen. My mom doesn't even like to cook for our family, and we have two kids, not three hundred.

The bell rang. It was time to line up and go back to Miss Daisy's class. Recess is way too short. We hardly had any chance to play.

I had forgotten what happened to Emily in the vomitorium, but the girls were still talking about it when we got back to class. Emily had apple juice on her clothes, and she looked upset, like her hamster died or something.

"It was all *your* fault, A.J.," said Andrea.

"My fault?" I said. "*You're* the one who knocked the apple juice over."

"You shot a straw at my head!" Andrea said.

"I did not," I said. "I shot a straw *wrapper* at your head. There's a big difference."

"Well, you're not invited to my birthday

party," Andrea said.

"I wouldn't go to your stupid birthday party even if I *was* invited," I said. Nah-nah-nah boo-boo on her.

Clap-clap, clap-clap-clap!

Miss Daisy clapped her hands, which means that everybody has to stop talking.

"I was going to start a unit about ancient Egypt today, but first I have some exciting news," Miss Daisy said. "Ella

Mentry School has won an award. Our school has been named the cleanest school in the district! Next week a special guest is coming to present us with the award."

"Oooh, who is it?" everybody asked.

"It's Ella Mentry!"

Ella Mentry! She's the lady our school was named after! On the front lawn there's a big sign that says "Ella Mentry Elementary School." There's a framed picture of her outside the front office, too. She looks like she's about a hundred million years old.

I thought Ella Mentry was dead, but Miss Daisy told us she's not only alive, but she lives just a few blocks away.

ELLA MENTRY

"Ella Mentry was a student at this school a long time ago," Miss Daisy said. "She went on to become a teacher here, and she taught students like you for thirty years."

"That's a long time to have the same teacher," I said. Everybody laughed even though I didn't say anything funny.

"Did she teach Abraham Lincoln?" Ryan asked.

"I don't know," said Miss Daisy, who

doesn't know anything. "Maybe we can ask Mrs. Mentry when she comes to visit."

Miss Daisy went to the chalkboard and wrote, "Did you teach Abraham Lincoln?"

"Maybe we can do something to honor Ella Mentry when she comes to visit," said Andrea Young, who's always trying to think of ways to do more work. Andrea will even ask for *more* homework.

"That's a great idea!" said Miss Daisy.

"How about we honor her by taking the day off from school?" I suggested. "That's how we honor Martin Luther King Jr."

"Mrs. Mentry wouldn't be very happy

to show up and find there are no children here," Miss Daisy said. "She loves kids."

"If she *really* loved kids, she would let us have the day off from school," I said.

Miss Smarty-pants Andrea was waving her hand in the air and moaning "Oooh . . . oooh . . . oooh" like she had to go to the bathroom.

"I have an idea," Andrea said. "We can make posters and banners and write letters to Ella Mentry."

I hate her. Why can't a safe drop on her head, like in the cartoons?

"That sounds marvelous!" said Miss Daisy, who loves all of Andrea's dumb ideas that involve us doing more work.

We had been learning how to write letters anyway, so Miss Daisy had us all write a letter to Ella Mentry. Writing letters is hard. I didn't know what to say.

We had to stand up and read our letters in front of the class. Andrea wrote a letter saying how excited she was that Ella Mentry was coming to visit. She said it must be really neat to have a school named after you, and that we were going to be on our best behavior for her. What a brownnoser!

I was hoping Miss Daisy would forget to call my name, but she didn't. So I had to stand up in the front of everybody and read.

Dear Mrs. Mentry,

My name is A.J. and I hate school. But I'm glad they named our school after you. Old people always forget things, like their names. But you can never forget your name, because every time you walk by our school, you see it in big letters. When I get old, I hope they name a skate park or a football stadium after me instead of a school. I wouldn't want my name on a place where kids are tortured all day.

Sincerely,

A.J.

*P.S.: If you want, when you come
visit I will burp the alphabet for
you. Ryan says he can do it, but
when he tried, he threw up.*

It was almost three o'clock. Miss Daisy said she would drop our letters off at Ella Mentry's house after school. Somebody asked if the lunch lady really quit or would she be back tomorrow. Miss Daisy said it was true that Mrs. McGillicuddy was not coming back.

"What are we gonna do?" Ryan asked. "If we don't have a lunch lady, there will be no lunch. You can't have lunch without a lunch lady. We'll starve and die!"

"We've got to do something!" said Emily, and she went running out of the room. Emily is weird.

"Oh, don't worry," Miss Daisy said. "I hear we're going to have a very special lunch lady tomorrow."

The New Lunch Lady

In the morning before school, I filled my backpack with all the stuff I would need during the day—cookies, chips, candy, pretzels, and other junk food. Miss Daisy always says we should be prepared. I wanted to be prepared in case there was no lunch lady. I didn't want to starve and die.

It was hard to concentrate all morning when we were doing math and DEAR. That stands for Drop Everything And Read. I was trying to read a book about jet planes, but I couldn't stop thinking about all the great food I had in my backpack.

In social studies we started learning about the pyramids and ancient Egypt. Did you know that when people died back then, they would take their brains out through their noses and turn them into mummies? It's true!

I was glad I brought stuff from home to eat. Because I'm sure that if I starved and died at school, Andrea would try to take

my brain out through my nose and turn
me into a mummy.

After social studies we started making
a big banner for Ella Mentry. It said

"Welcome, Ella Mentry," and we spent the rest of the morning drawing little pictures all over it.

"What do you think the new lunch lady will be like?" somebody asked as we worked on the banner.

"I hope she's nice," Emily said.

"She's got to be nicer than Mrs. McGillicuddy," Ryan said.

I wasn't thinking about the new lunch lady. I kept thinking about those mummies in Egypt. I decided I will never pick my nose again. I don't want to pull my brain out by accident.

Finally Miss Daisy sang the cleanup song and said it was time for the cleanest school in the district to get ready for lunch.

"Yay!" everybody yelled.

We washed our hands and lined up in size order. Then we walked in single file to the vomitorium. Andrea was the line leader. We all walked really fast because we couldn't wait to meet the new lunch lady.

"I hope she doesn't make those rubber hot dogs like Mrs. McGillicuddy," Ryan said.

"Or those chicken nuggets that bounce," said Michael.

"Or the nachos that glow in the dark," I added.

"People who want to lose weight should come to our school," Ryan said. "Because once you take a look at the food, you never want to eat again."

"A little less chitchatting please," Miss Daisy said.

Miss Daisy doesn't eat with us in the vomitorium. She eats in the teachers' lounge, which is a secret clubhouse where the teachers put on bathing suits and eat in a big hot tub. I hear they have a disco ball, too. In the vomitorium the other grown-ups are on lunch duty, like Ms. Hannah, the art teacher; Mr. Docker, the science teacher; Miss Small, the gym teacher; and Mr. Loring, the music teacher. They stand around and tell us to stop talking.

After walking a million hundred miles, we got to the vomitorium. We were finally going to meet the new lunch lady.

Andrea opened the door.

We rushed inside.

It was so exciting!

Standing at the door, with an apron and gloves on, was the new lunch lady.

It was Mr. Klutz, the principal!

Chicken Klutz

"Mr. Klutz! What are *you* doing here?" I asked.

"Are you the new lunch lady?" asked Andrea.

"I'm the lunch, uh, person for *today*," Mr. Klutz said. "The new lunch lady is Ms. LaGrange. She starts tomorrow."

Mr. Klutz looked funny. He was wearing a lunch lady hairnet, which was really weird because he doesn't have any hair at all. His head is like a beach ball. It looked like a beach ball in a net.

Mr. Klutz showed us something new that he installed in the middle of the vomitorium to help us be quiet—a traffic light on a big pole. When the light is green, he told us, we're allowed to talk. When it's yellow, we can whisper. And when it's red, we have "silent lunch."

Usually during lunch everybody is yelling and screaming. You have to scream just to be heard over the other kids who are screaming so they can be heard. And then you have to scream even louder. It just goes on and on. Maybe the traffic light would help.

Mr. Klutz told us he loves to cook at home, and he made all the food himself. Little Miss Perfect Andrea said she and her mother cook together all the time.

"We only eat organic food at home," Andrea said.

"You eat organs?" I asked. "That's disgusting!"

There was a chalkboard that listed all the foods Mr. Klutz had made for us: macaroni and cheese . . . tuna casserole . . . meat loaf . . .

"What's that stuff?" I asked, pointing at some mystery meat covered in brown goo.

"That's an old family recipe," said Mr. Klutz. "I call it chicken Klutz."

I call it disgusting. But I didn't say that out loud.

"The only chicken I eat is chicken nuggets," I said.

"Chicken Klutz is *real* chicken," Mr. Klutz said. "Try it, A.J."

"Does it have bones in it?"

"Of course!" Mr. Klutz said. "Chickens have bones, just like people."

I told Mr. Klutz I wasn't hungry. I didn't want to hurt his feelings by telling him his chicken looked like somebody threw up on it. I got a carton of chocolate milk and sat at a table with Ryan and Michael.

I opened my backpack and dumped the cookies, chips, candy, pretzels, and other junk food on the table.

Everybody got all excited. Even Andrea and her annoying friends turned around so they could witness my awesomely cool lunch, live and in person.

"You should eat smarter," Andrea said. "Proper nutrition is important for learning, growth, and development."

"Can you possibly be any more boring?" I asked her.

After everybody got their food, Mr. Klutz walked around the vomitorium. He was carrying a platter with some disgusting green stuff on it. I was eating a candy bar when he came over to our table.

"I thought you said you weren't hungry, A.J.," he said. "Why are you eating sugary treats?"

I didn't know what to say. I didn't know what to do. I had to think fast.

"I'm on the new all-sugar diet," I told him. "Haven't you heard of it? You're only allowed to eat sugar. It's the latest thing."

"A.J.," Mr. Klutz said, "you know your body needs protein, fruits, vegetables, and grains. Haven't you heard of the food groups?"

"But I don't *like* that stuff," I said.

"Fruit is sweet," he said. "You *must* have a favorite fruit, right?"

"Sure I do," I replied. "Froot Loops."

"Come on, A.J.!" he said, picking up a spoonful of his disgusting green stuff off his platter. "How about some peas and carrots? Have you ever tasted peas? They're delicious. And carrots are good for your eyes."

"I'd rather go blind than eat carrots," I said.

Mr. Klutz looked pretty upset. I guess he was sad because hardly anybody ordered his chicken Klutz. He'd have to bring it home in a doggie bag. That's what my parents do when they have leftovers.

Mr Klutz should stick to being principal, if you ask me. He makes a terrible lunch lady.

France Talk and Frogs' Legs

The next day there was a sign in front of the school: "Welcome, Ms. LaGrange!"

Mr. Klutz was standing at the front door next to a lady I never saw before. Her hair stuck out from under a big chef's hat, and she was wearing an apron with the words "Make Lunch, Not War" on it.

"Ms. LaGrange, this is A.J.," Mr. Klutz

said when I reached the top of the steps. "Maybe you can get him to eat some vegetables."

"*Bonjour*, Mr. A.J.," said Ms. LaGrange.

"You talk funny," I said.

"Ms. LaGrange comes from France," Mr. Klutz told me. "*Bonjour* means 'hello' in French."

"Well, *bonjour* to you, too," I said.

When we got to class, everybody was talking about Ms. LaGrange, the new lunch lady.

"Miss Daisy, where is France?" asked Andrea.

"I have no idea," said Miss Daisy, who never knows anything. I wonder how she ever got a job as a teacher.

Miss Daisy pulled down a big map of the world. We looked all over the map until we found France. It was on the other side of the Atlantic Ocean.

"Did Ms. LaGrange swim to school?" asked Emily. What a dumbhead!

"She probably took an airplane," said Miss Daisy.

"If she took an airplane, she should give it back," I said. Nobody laughed at my joke even though it was funny.

We were supposed to work on our "Welcome, Ella Mentry" banner, but Miss Daisy let us use the computers to go on the Internet and learn more about France.

We learned all kinds of things. Did you know that France gave us the Statue of

Liberty? I guess they didn't want it. When my mom has stuff that she doesn't want, she gives it away. Or sometimes she just throws it in the garbage.

Ryan found out that in France they eat snails and frogs' legs. I thought I was gonna throw up.

"What do they do with the *rest* of the frog?" Michael asked.

"Ms. LaGrange will probably serve it for lunch," Ryan said.

I said I like French food, like French fries and French toast.

"You silly dumbhead," Andrea said.

"French fries aren't French."

"Are too!"

"Are not."

We went back and forth like that for a while until Miss Daisy asked if anyone knew anything else about France.

"I know a poem about France," I said.

"Oh, will you share it with us, A.J.?"

So I said my poem:

"I see London, I see France
I see Emily's underpants."

Emily got up and ran out of the room crying. What is her problem? It was just a poem.

After we learned everything about

France, we learned more about ancient Egypt. Miss Daisy showed us pictures of the pyramids. They were cool. Then she said it was time for math, even though she doesn't know anything about math. She can't even add or subtract, so *we* have to teach *her*. Miss Daisy begged us not to tell Mr. Klutz how dumb she is because she doesn't want to be fired.

Miss Daisy is crazy!

Finally it was time for lunch with Ms. LaGrange. We were so excited!

Welcome to Café LaGrange

When we walked into the vomitorium, it looked completely different. I thought that maybe we were in the wrong place.

The lights were turned down so low you could hardly see. There was a sign in the corner that said "Café LaGrange." The tables were covered with tablecloths and fake candles that were really electric lights. There was even music! A few of the fifth graders in the orchestra were playing violins. It sounded like the noise you make when you pinch the end of a balloon and let the air out.

"Oooh!" Emily said. "It's beautiful! It's like going to a fancy restaurant."

If there's one thing I hate more than school and vegetables, it's going to fancy restaurants. But I didn't say anything. We were all on our best behavior because we wanted to make a good impression on Ms. LaGrange.

"Wait until Ella Mentry comes to our school and sees *this*," Andrea said. "She's going to be really impressed."

Suddenly Ms. LaGrange came out of the kitchen.

"Bonjour!" she said in that French talk. "Welcome to Café LaGrange."

"Bonjour," we all said back.

"The specials of the day are French Sloppy Joe sandwiches, French salisbury steak, French chili surprise, and French tuna casserole," said Ms. LaGrange.

"It sounds yummy!" said Andrea, who compliments grown-ups no matter what they do.

We got in line. It all looked like the same old disgusting foods to me, except that they had the word "French" in front of them.

"Do you have any French peanut

butter and jelly sandwiches?" I asked. Whoever invented the peanut butter and jelly sandwich was a genius.

"No, but I have French mashed potatoes," Ms. LaGrange said.

I looked at the mashed potatoes. They looked pretty normal, except for one thing. There were letters written in them. The letters were *Y-A-W-Y-E*. It didn't even spell a word.

"Ms. LaGrange, what does 'YAWYE' mean?" asked Ryan.

"Oh, that is my little secret," she replied. "Maybe I will tell you someday. Who would like to try French peas and carrots?"

"Me! Me! Me!" said Andrea, who loves every horrible-tasting thing that's good for you.

"Not me," I said.

"Did you ever *try* peas or carrots, Mister A.J.?"

"No."

"Well, how do you know you don't like them if you don't try them?" she asked.

"I never tried eating dirt," I said, "but I'm pretty sure I wouldn't like that."

"Won't you *please* try my peas and carrots, Mister A.J.," she said. "Pretty please?"

"No!"

Suddenly Ms. LaGrange picked up one of those spray bottles that lunch ladies use to clean off the tables. She pointed it at me. Then she squirted water in my face!

"Hey!" I shouted. "What's the big idea?"

"Anyone who refuses to try peas and carrots will be sprayed," said Ms. LaGrange.

Everybody else took some peas and carrots. The yellow traffic light was on, so we were allowed to whisper at our tables.

"Ms. LaGrange is strange," I said as I wiped off my face.

"Yeah," Ryan agreed. "What's the deal with those mashed potatoes? What do you think 'YAWYE' means?"

We all thought about it.

"I know what it means," Michael said. "You Always Wash Your Ears."

"Maybe it means Yes Always Wipe Your Elbows," guessed Ryan.

"I know," I said. "Young Adults Want Yellow Elephants."

"That makes no sense at all," Michael

said, throwing one of his Tater Tots at me.

We were still trying to figure out what 'YAWYE' meant when Ms. LaGrange came around from table to table with one of those big pepper shakers.

"Are you *sure* you won't try my French

peas and carrots, Mister A.J.?" she asked.

"If I say no, are you going to brain me with that pepper thing?" I asked.

"Of course not," she replied. "But you know, A.J., carrots are good for your eyes. You never saw a rabbit wearing glasses, did you?"

"I never saw a bird wearing glasses either," I replied, "but that doesn't mean I'm gonna eat worms."

Andrea and her annoying friends at the next table turned around.

"I bet you'd like baby carrots, A.J.," Andrea said. "They're yummy!"

"Do you know where baby carrots come from?" asked Ms. LaGrange.

"Baby carrots grow out of the ground!" Andrea said.

"That's disgusting," I said. "Food comes in cans and jars and boxes, not out of the ground! I'm not going to eat something that grew in dirt!"

"Americans are silly," said Ms. LaGrange. "In France I grew my own food in a garden behind my house. Say, maybe we can start a vegetable garden out by the playground, so you can learn where food comes from."

"That would be wonderful!" said Andrea. "We can work in the garden during recess."

Oh, great. We get twenty minutes all

day to run around, and we'll have to spend that time digging in the dirt for yucky vegetables.

I think Ms. LaGrange saw me wrinkle up my nose, because she said she likes sugary treats, just like me. She said she has a special treat in the freezer, and she's going to wait for a special occasion to give it to us.

Ugh. It's probably dead frogs with no legs.

Secret Agents

After lunch we had social studies. Miss Daisy showed us a video about the pyramids in Egypt. She said that when the pyramids were built, they didn't have trucks or cranes or machines. And each of those rocks weighed over a thousand pounds.

"How did they pick them up?" I asked.

"I have no idea," said Miss Daisy, who doesn't know anything.

We spent the rest of the afternoon working on our "Welcome, Ella Mentry" banner. She was coming to visit any day.

Finally the little hand on the clock reached three and the big hand reached twelve. Three o'clock. Hooray! I walked home with Ryan and Michael.

"Those pyramids are cool," I said. "How do you think they picked up those big rocks?"

"It's a mystery," said Ryan.

"The big mystery is that secret code Ms. LaGrange writes in the mashed potatoes," Michael said. "We have to figure out what 'YAWYE' means."

"Maybe it means You All Wet Your Envelopes," suggested Ryan.

"Maybe it means Yes We Have No Bananas," I suggested.

"That would be *Y-W-H-N-B*, dumbhead," said Michael.

"Close enough," I said.

"Maybe Ms. LaGrange isn't a lunch lady at all," Michael said. "Did you ever think of that?"

"What do you mean?" asked Ryan.

"Maybe she's a fake," Michael said. "Maybe she kidnapped our *real* new lunch lady and locked her in the freezer.

Stuff like that happens all the time, you know."

"My friend Billy around the corner told me they freeze dead people so they can bring them back to life in the future," I said.

"Your friend Billy is weird," said Ryan.

"I bet our real lunch lady is in the freezer," I said.

"Along with Ms. LaGrange's special dessert," Michael said.

"And the secret of YAWYE," added Ryan.

That's when I got the most genius idea in the history of the world—we should go back to school and see what was in the freezer!

You know me. I don't like going to school in the morning. I sure didn't like the idea of going *back* at the end of the day. But we all agreed that this was important. We had to save the frozen lunch lady. We had to find the secret of

YAWYE. And we had to get a taste of that special dessert Ms. LaGrange was hiding.

So we went back to school.

The side door near the vomitorium was open. We tiptoed inside. Nobody was around. We pretended we were secret agents. We snuck into the back of the kitchen.

"There's the freezer!" Ryan said.

We made sure no grown-ups were around, and then we pulled open the door. The freezer was so big you could walk into it. We could see our breath.

"This is cool," I said, stepping inside.

"It's cooler than cool," said Ryan. "It's freezing!"

It was dark in the freezer. I didn't see any frozen lunch ladies or special desserts. There were just a bunch of big boxes.

"Let's get out of here," Michael said. "This place is—"

That's when the door slammed shut. Everything went completely dark. We were stuck in there!

The Most Horrible, Terrible, Awful Thing in the History of the World

8

We couldn't see a thing! We didn't know where the light switch was! We didn't know where the door handle was! We were trapped!

"Oh no!" said Michael.

"How are we gonna get out?" Ryan asked. "School is closed! Everybody went home!"

"We're gonna turn into icicles!" said Michael.

"My friend Billy told me about this ice man guy they found in Italy," I said. "He was frozen solid for a thousand years."

"Help! Help!" we screamed. We pounded on the door with our fists.

"Somebody help!" Ryan shouted. "We're locked in the freezer!"

We must have been in there for a million hundred minutes, when suddenly the door opened.

Ms. LaGrange was standing there.

"What are you boys doing in here?"

I didn't know what to say. I didn't know what to do. I had to think fast.

"Bonjour," I said. "We were looking for

the boys' bathroom."

"Well, this isn't it," she said. "Come out of there. You'll freeze your tootsies off."

Ms. LaGrange was really nice. She made us hot chocolate and promised that she wouldn't tell anyone we were sneaking around the freezer. And she made us promise we would never go near the freezer again.

I thought that nothing could be worse than getting trapped in the freezer. But when I got home from school, the most horrible, terrible, awful thing in the history of the world happened.

The mailman came. My mom went through the mail. She told me there was a envelope for me. I opened it up. There was a card inside. This is what it said. . . .

YOU ARE INVITED TO ANDREA'S
BIRTHDAY PARTY!

Give Peas a Chance

"I'm not going."

"You have to go."

Just my luck. My mother and Andrea's mother are friends. They met when me and Andrea were in preschool together. They even play tennis with each other. So I would have to go to Andrea's stupid birthday party.

I looked at the invitation again.

YOU ARE INVITED TO ANDREA'S
BIRTHDAY PARTY!
IT'S A TEA PARTY!

A tea party? What kind of a dumb birthday party is *that*? Kids are supposed to have bowling parties or skating parties or movie parties. Who wants to go to a party and drink tea? I hate tea.

The first thing I did when I got to school the next day was to find Andrea. She was at her cubby putting her backpack away.

"I thought you said you weren't going to invite me to your birthday party," I whispered to her.

"I didn't *want* to invite you," she said. "My mother made me."

"Well, I'm not going," I said.

"Good."

Ryan and Michael were goofing around by the water fountain.

"Hey, are you guys going to Andrea's tea party?" I asked.

"What tea party?" asked Ryan.

"I'd rather die," Michael said. "Why, are you invited?"

"Uh, no," I lied. "I was just wondering." I didn't want Michael and Ryan to know Andrea invited me to her party.

"So how did *you* know Andrea was having a tea party?" Michael asked.

"I don't know," I said.

If you're ever stuck for an answer and you don't know what to say, just say "I don't know." It works every time. Well, almost every time.

"A.J., you were invited to Andrea's party, weren't you?" asked Ryan.

"No."

"I saw you whispering to Andrea," Michael said. "Hey, everybody, A.J.'s going to a tea party!"

"I am not!"

"Oooh!" Ryan said. "A.J. and Andrea are in *love*!"

"When are you gonna get married?" asked Michael.

If those guys weren't my best friends, I would hate them.

Fortunately Miss Daisy clapped her hands to shut everybody up. We pledged the allegiance, and then we learned some more about ancient Egypt. Miss Daisy asked if anybody figured out how they picked up those big rocks to build the pyramids. Nobody raised their hand. Then we worked on our "Welcome, Ella Mentry" banner until lunchtime.

When I got to the front of the lunch line, Ms. LaGrange winked at me.

"You look cold, Mister A.J.," she said. "Like you've been in a freezer. How about some nice hot French peas and

72

carrots to warm you up?"

"No, thanks."

"Oh, come on," she said, grabbing for her squirt bottle. "Give peas a chance."

Ms. LaGrange didn't squirt me with her squirt bottle. She did something even weirder. She started singing!

"All we are saying, is give peas a chance."

And then she sang it again, really loud.

"All we are saying, is give peas a chance."

It was a really annoying song, but the next thing I knew, all the teachers joined in.

"All we are saying, is give peas a chance."

Then the whole lunchroom was singing that stupid pea song! It was totally embarrassing. It almost made me want to eat some peas just to shut them up.

"I'll tell you what," I said to Ms. LaGrange. "If I eat a pea, will you tell me what 'YAWYE' means?"

She was thinking it over.

"Just one pea?" she asked.

"Yeah, one pea."

...all we are saying is give peas a chance...

"Okay," she agreed. "Let's see you eat one pea, Mister A.J."

Everybody started cheering.

Ms. LaGrange picked up a pea with a spoon. She held it up to my mouth.

Everybody started clapping.

I closed my eyes. I opened my mouth.

Everybody started chanting, "A.J.! A.J.! A.J.!"

And I ate the pea.

It wasn't bad, to tell you the truth. At least I didn't throw up.

"Okay," I said, after swallowing the pea, "what does 'YAWYE' mean?"

"'YAWYE,'" Ms. LaGrange said, "stands for You Are What You Eat."

A.J. A.J. A.J.

"You are what you eat?" I asked.

"That's right," she said. "If you eat good, healthy food, you'll be a good, healthy person. And if you eat junk, well . . ."

I thought about that for a moment.

"I'm a pea!" I screamed. "Ugh, it's disgusting! I'm going to die!"

Andrea's Birthday Party

I told my mom I was sick from eating a pea, but she said I had to go to Andrea's birthday party anyway. She even made me dress up like a grown-up in a jacket and tie. It was horrible.

When Mom dropped me off at Andrea's house, she made me promise to behave and handed me a present she had bought for Andrea. I went up the steps and rang the doorbell.

"I'm so glad to see you, A.J.," said Andrea's mother, who looks just like Andrea but with wrinkles.

"I thought you said you weren't coming," said Andrea.

"My mother made me," I said, handing her the present.

I saw Emily and a few other girls in our class. It took me about two seconds to realize something horrible. Of all the kids at Andrea's party, I was the only boy. *The only boy!* There were all these giggly girls running around Andrea's living room in party dresses. It was awful.

I went into the kitchen. Maybe at least they'd have some good junk food to eat, I figured. But you'll never guess in a million years who was standing at the stove in the kitchen.

It was Ms. LaGrange!

"Bonjour, Mister A.J.!" she said. "You look very handsome in a jacket and tie!"

"Ms. LaGrange, what are *you* doing here?"

"I'm the caterer," she said.

"So you made the food?"

"We."

"We?" I asked. "You and who else?

"No," she said. "*We* means 'yes' in French."

That didn't make any sense to me.

"If *we* means 'yes,'" I asked, "how do you say 'we'?"

"We?"

"Yes," I said. "How do you say 'we'?"

"We," she said.

"But you said *we* means 'yes,'" I said. "It can't also mean 'we.'"

"No?"

Oh, forget it. That French talk makes no sense at all.

"Did you make any junk food?" I asked.

"Junk food?" said Ms. LaGrange. "Oh, no. Remember YAWYE? You are what you eat."

The party was the most boring party in the history of the world. Ms. LaGrange made a bunch of weird French foods that don't even exist in America. I almost ate this thing called escargot until Ms. LaGrange told me it was a snail.

I almost ate a snail! I thought I was gonna throw up.

"Isn't trying new foods fun, A.J.?" Andrea's mother asked.

"Oh, yeah," I lied. "Lots of fun. Are we gonna play some games or something?"

"Games?" Andrea's mother asked. "What kind of games?"

"You know, like when you whack a piñata with a baseball bat until it busts and all the candy falls out," I said.

"That sounds rather violent," Andrea's

mother said. "In this house we don't believe in hitting."

I was so bored. I kept waiting for something to happen, but nothing ever did! Everybody just sat there eating snails and drinking tea. There was nothing for me to do.

I noticed a little garbage can in the corner. I decided to see if I could throw one of those snail things into the garbage can from across the room. So I picked one up and threw it at the garbage can.

The only problem was, Emily was standing next to the garbage can. Instead of hitting the garbage can, I hit Emily. In the head.

She fell backward and landed on a little table that had a bunch of teacups on it. The teacups went flying everywhere. Emily was on the floor, freaking out. Man, she falls down a lot.

"There's tea all over my shirt!" Emily screamed.

"Now it's a tea shirt!" I said. "Ha-ha-ha!"

I thought that was pretty funny, but nobody laughed. Girls have no sense of humor at all.

"I bumped my mouth!" Emily shouted. "I think my loose tooth is going to fall out!"

What a crybaby. Her dumb tooth was going to fall out anyway. What was the big deal?

Finally the horrible party was over, and my mom came to pick me up. On the way out, Ms. LaGrange handed me a goody bag. You'll never guess in a million hundred years what was in it.

Tea bags!

That had to be the dumbest party in the history of the world. The only good thing about it was that Andrea probably won't invite me to her birthday party next year.

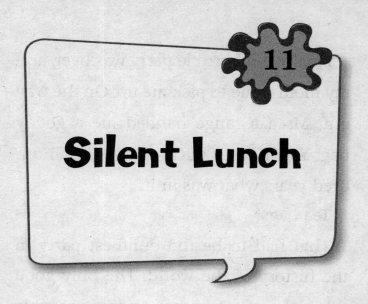

Silent Lunch

It was the next day. The green traffic light was on in the vomitorium.

"How was Andrea's party, A.J.?" Ryan asked me, poking Michael in the side and giggling.

"It was cool," I lied. "There was a rock climbing wall and a half pipe for skateboarding. At the end I got a goody bag, and there was a remote control car in it."

No way I was going to tell them I sat around drinking tea with Andrea and her friends.

While we were talking, I was playing with my fork and spoon on the table. And when I put my spoon across my fork, the most amazing thing in the history of the world happened.

"I figured it out!" I shouted.

"Figured what out?" asked Ryan and Michael.

"I just figured out how the Egyptians picked up those big rocks to build the pyramids!"

"How?"

"Look," I said, scooping up some of Ryan's carrots and peas with my spoon. "Imagine these peas and carrots are big rocks. Nobody could pick one up. But if they could slide them onto a big scoop like this, and put the scoop across a big fork like this, it would be easier to pick up."

I put the spoonful of carrots and peas across my fork, like the spoon and fork were a little seesaw.

"You're right!" Michael said, smashing his fist down on the table.

The only problem was, Michael's fist missed the table and hit the long end of the spoon instead. The peas and carrots went flying up in the air. They hit the ceiling and then . . . they stuck up there!

The ceiling was splotched with peas and carrots. It was the coolest thing in the history of the world! You should have been there!

Me and Ryan and Michael looked up at the ceiling. We were excited that I had solved the mystery of the pyramids.

That's when Miss I Know Everything came over to our table. She looked all mad.

"A.J.," Andrea said, "you ruined my birthday party!"

"I did not!"

"Did too!"

We went back and forth like that a few more times, but then something totally amazing happened. Remember those peas and carrots that were stuck to the ceiling? Well, I guess they didn't stick very well, because they started falling down—on Andrea's head!

"Eeeeeek!" Andrea screamed. "I can't see! I've got carrots in my eyes!"

"That's okay, Andrea," I said. "Carrots are *good* for your eyes!"

Ryan and Michael thought that was hilarious, but I guess Andrea didn't. She picked up Michael's bowl of spaghetti and dumped it over my head.

Nobody dumps spaghetti over my head and gets away with it. I picked up Ryan's bowl of macaroni and cheese and pushed it in Andrea's face.

"Food fight! Food fight!" everybody started chanting.

I'm not exactly sure what happened next. Things sort of went out of control.

Kids started shouting and throwing stuff at each other. Mr. Klutz turned on the red light, but it didn't help.

"This is a silent lunch!" Mr. Klutz

shouted. But it was so loud in there that you could hardly hear him.

Pickle chips were flying around. Somebody got hold of Ms. LaGrange's pepper shaker and started hitting meatballs up in the air like they were baseballs. Emily got hit in the head with a meatball, and the big crybaby freaked out.

"Help, help!" she screamed. "My tooth fell out! I think I swallowed it. I'm choking!"

Emily got up to run out of the room, but instead she crashed right into the big traffic light. It toppled over. As it was falling, the traffic light hit our "Welcome, Ella Mentry" banner and ripped it in half. *Crash!*

It was at that moment that the door to the vomitorium opened. You'll never guess in a million years who walked in.

It was Ella Mentry!

Everybody stopped what they were doing. Nobody made a sound.

Ella Mentry limped into the vomitorium. She held a cane in one hand. In her other hand she held the plaque we won for having the cleanest school in the district.

I looked at Ms. LaGrange. Ms. LaGrange looked at Ella Mentry. Ella Mentry looked around the vomitorium.

"Welcome to Ella Mentry School!" said Mr. Klutz, coming over to greet her. "We are proud and honored—"

Mr. Klutz never got the chance to finish his sentence. Ella Mentry picked up some kid's chocolate pudding and dumped it over Mr. Klutz's head!

"I always wanted to do that," Ella Mentry said.

"Well," Mr. Klutz said, licking the pudding off his face. "I guess lunch is on me!"

Mr. Klutz is nuts!

The next thing anyone knew, food was flying through the air again. Mrs. Cooney, the nurse, hit our music teacher, Mr. Loring, with a beef and bean burrito. Ms. Hannah, the art teacher, threw a plate full of chili surprise at our librarian, Mrs. Roopy. Miss Small, the gym teacher, hit our science teacher, Mr. Docker, with a corn dog.

It was raining Tater Tots! Kids were squirting ketchup packets at each other. Somebody was running around spraying people with Ms. LaGrange's spray bottle.

"I haven't had this much fun in years!"

Ella Mentry said as she picked up a chicken potpie and heaved it across the vomitorium.

Ella Mentry is weird.

I guess Mr. Klutz can't say that we don't get enough exercise anymore. With all the throwing and ducking and running around, food fights are great exercise.

Eventually we ran out of food to throw at each other. When it was all over, Café LaGrange was a mess. All the food groups were stuck to the wall.

"Maybe I should go back to France, no?" Ms. LaGrange said.

Miss Lazar, the custodian, came in with her mop.

"Oh, great," she said. "A mess. I love cleaning up messes."

"Don't clean it up!" shouted Ms. Hannah, our art teacher. "It's not a mess. This is art!"

Ms. Hannah is bananas!

Everybody got quiet when Ella Mentry cleared her throat to talk.

"Where is the boy who wrote me a letter saying he hated school?"

Everybody looked at me. I didn't know what to say. I didn't know what to do. I had to think fast.

So I started burping—*A-B-C-D-E-F-G-H-I-J-K-L-M-N-O-P* . . .

When I finished burping the alphabet, the whole school gave me a standing ovation. Ella Mentry gave me a hug. She said that when she was a student here, she hated school too.

"But coming back to Ella Mentry School was the most fun I ever had in my life. Thank you."

To celebrate, Ms. LaGrange brought out the special dessert she was hiding in the freezer. It was called sorbet. It's sort of a cross between ice cream and water ice. Yum! While we were eating it, Emily found her tooth. It was right on her plate. What a dumbhead!

As it turned out, we didn't get to keep the award for having the cleanest school in the district. Somebody at the board of education found out about the food fight, and they gave the award to some other school instead.

Mr. Klutz said that if we clean up the vomitorium and work really hard to control ourselves, maybe next year we'll have the cleanest school in the district.

But it won't be easy!